Max and Maurice

and other picture- stories

Wilhelm Busch 著

陸谷孫 譯

© 100% 頑童手記
Max and Maurice

著作人	Wilhelm Busch
譯 者	陸谷孫
發行人	劉振強
著作財產權人	三民書局股份有限公司
	臺北市復興北路三八六號
發行所	三民書局股份有限公司
	地 址／臺北市復興北路三八六號
	郵 撥／○○○九九九八一五號
印刷所	三民書局股份有限公司
門市部	復北店／臺北市復興北路三八六號
	重南店／臺北市重慶南路一段六十一號
初 版	中華民國八十五年三月

編 號 S 88001

基本定價 肆元

行政院新聞局登記證局版臺業字第○二○○號

ISBN 957-14-2460-9 （精裝）

維爾翰·布希小傳

(WILHELM BUSCH)

　　維爾翰·布希(WILHELM BUSCH)為一德國畫家和作家，1832年□月十五日生於 Wiednsahl（位於漢諾瓦），1908 年一月九日歿於echtshausen。曾參加杜塞道夫(Dusseldorf)、安特衛普(Antwerpen)及尼黑(Munchen)協會，1898年退休。維爾翰·布希為德國通俗幽默作□，其影響在於他能準確的結合滑稽、簡單的雙行押韻詩，和尖銳、□明的插圖。他的畫風也頗具諷刺性，處理畫作時，喜揭穿自以為是、□道學和虛偽的虔誠。維爾翰·布希亦創造了哲理性的抒情詩及散文，□方面是特別受到叔本華(Arthur Schopenhauer)的影響。

Index

麥克斯和毛里斯
Max and Maurice   *1*
蒼蠅
The Fly   *87*
鴉巢
The Raven's Nest   *97*
狄俄涅斯和科林斯的男孩
Diogenes and the Boys of Corinth   *105*
兩隻鴨子和青蛙
The Two Ducks and the Frog   *115*
艾琴哈和艾瑪
Eginhard and Emma   *123*

Prologue

Of naughty boys to hear or read
Is often very sad indeed.
This evil pair, called Max and Maurice,
Also gave rise to wicked stories.

Instead of listening to the teachers
To mend their ways, these naughty creatures
Just laughed at all that those did say,
And went their own malicious way.
To make some bad and evil trick
Those boys were never getting sick.
Teasing animals and men
Was their favourite pastime then,
Stealing apples, pears and plums
They were champions, these two chums.
For them a boy was just a fool,
Who would sit still in church and school.
But you will see the fearful end,
To what disaster their lives tend.
No one will probably deplore,
What fortune had for them in store.
Therefore what they did in those times,
Is pictured here and put in rhymes.

開場白

聽故事，讀話本，
事關頑童引人常悲憤。
說一對這樣刁惡的壞孩子，
名叫麥克斯和毛里斯。

教師告誡當耳邊風，
金玉良言遭嘲弄。
行為不端愛調皮，
頑童無日不淘氣。
玩弄惡作劇手法新，
捉狹念頭無窮盡。
虐待動物，逗弄他人，
此種消遣最娛人。
偷摘水果上樹忙，
一身絕技再無雙。
哪個童子禮拜讀書守規矩，
定被他倆斥迂愚。
但是讀者諸君耐心看，
頑童的下場何其凶險！
造化弄人早有定，
作惡多端無人憫。
頑童劣跡刊布於此，
押韻傳唱儆後世。

First Trick

惡作劇之一

Some people take a lot of pains
To rear their fowl with corn and grains.
They are a help in many a way,
Think only of the eggs they lay.

世人多好飼家禽，
餵穀供米好勤奮。
蛋類誠佳品，
可見家禽多功能。

A fine meal, eaten now and then,
Provides a roasted cock or hen.
At last their feathers may be used,
For no one feels himself amused
To lie in bed quite cool and cold,
He may be young or getting old.

時逢佳節食豐饒，
烤雞必定是佳餚。
禽死尚餘豐茂羽，
充作床墊將寒禦。
不管老少或青壯，
誰願僵臥貧寒床？

Look here, this is good Mrs. Bold,
She, too, did not enjoy the cold.

話說有位波德太太，
輕軟床墊同樣喜愛，

Nice hens she had, in number three,
And one proud cock was there, you see.

為此飼養三隻肥雞婆，
伴有趾高氣揚的雄雞成一窩。

Now Max and Maurice, just for fun,
Were thinking what there could be done.
And from a loaf, the naughty pair
Were cutting bread as you see there.
A finger's thickness was the size,
They chose for every little slice.
Now like a cross they knot a thread,
And bound on ends a piece of bread.
In Mrs. Bold's yard, then and there,
They placed the thread with utmost care.

麥克斯和毛里斯，
僅為取樂費心思。
兩個頑童一對寶，
取來一段圓棍麵包。
切得四片用於遊戲，
片片都像手指粗細。
再用細線結成十字，
四端綁紮麵包作誘餌。
庭院設機關，
巧布陷阱把戲玩。

When this the cock has got to know,
He hastens up, begins to crow:
Cock-cock-a-doddle-doddle-do !
They run along with much ado.

公雞發現有麵包，
快步趨前咕咕叫：
咯—咯—喔喔喔！
母雞聞聲急急趕來啄。

And greedily and without dread
They swallow each a piece of bread.

四雞貪食無戒備，
一雞一片麵包皆樂胃。

But soon they saw with greatest terror
That they had made a fatal error.

旋即發現大事不好，
鑄成大錯齊哀號。

This way and that they tried to sever,
To come apart all four could never.

一線已將四雞咽喉牽，
東奔西突掙脫全無效驗。

They fluttered up now in the air
In greatest need and in despair.

走投無路掙扎凶，
四雞拍翅騰半空。

Here on the branch of an old tree
They are now hanging as you see,

躍上老樹掛枝頭，
線串四雞頸脖抖。

And soon their necks get ever longer,
And so their shrieking ever stronger.

頸脖懸吊細又長，
聲聲尖嚎慘又響。

Behold! Before their last sad cry
Each lays an egg and then they die.

瞧！不等垂死一聲叫，
雞屁股各有一蛋往下掉。

Good Mrs. Bold in bed was lying,
When suddenly she heard their crying.

波德太太躺臥榻，
突聞淒慘雞聲聒。

Terrified she rushes out,
"Help!", was all that she could shout.

三腳兩步往外衝，
狂呼「救命！」聲驚恐。

"Oh, come forth, ye floods of tears!
All that comforts, all that cheers,

Life's finest dream, as you can see,
Is hanging on this apple-tree".

「呵，湧起吧，滔滔的淚！
一切歡樂，一切快慰，
生活最甜美的夢，
吊在蘋果樹上全葬送。」

With pity and in deep distress
She takes a knife in all this mess,
Releasing them from dangling there,
She once had reared with so much care.

痛惜交加心如煎，
取刀在手割吊線。
晃盪雞屍紛落地，
那可是辛勤餵養心血所繫。

And having now no other chance,
Goes back with sad and mournful glance.
This was all a nasty trick,
But the second follows quick.

事已至此無挽回，
只好留下一瞥苦又悲。
這場惡作劇令人生氣，
不料一波甫平一波又起。

Second Trick

When Mrs. Bold, half dead with woe,
Recovered from this dreadful blow,
At last she made her mind up that

She'd fry them all in sizzling fat,
Whose lives on earth, oh great good Lord,
Were only pitiful and short.
And then, whatever she may feel,
She'd eat them as a well cooked meal.
Of course, it was a mournful sight,
To see them naked in their plight,
And plucked of feathers lying cold,
Who in their prime and days of old
Were lively scratching in the sand,
In garden, yard, the merry band.
She weeps again, 'twas very bad,
Her little dog was also sad.
When Max and Maurice smelled the frying,
"Let's climb the roof", the two were crying.

惡作劇之二

波德太太心火急，
好不容易緩過氣。

上帝呵，家禽生命不足道，
活不長久歸陰曹。
雞死嘆息白費勁，
不如重油煎烹作佳品。
縱然心頭夠沈重，
烤雞噴香堪受用。
只是雞屍樣子夠可憐，
去毛裸露無尊嚴。
孰知正是這些雞，
無不有過壯年好運氣。
搔扒沙礫覓食忙，
活蹦亂跳庭院任遊蕩。
今昔一比，波德太太又揮淚，
連她的小狗也傷悲。
不料兩個頑童聞得烤雞香，
爬上屋頂又把計謀想。

And through the chimney with delight
The chickens could be seen all right,

登上煙囪口往下望，
喜上心頭頑童饞涎淌。

Which now were turning crisp and brown,
What fun the boys had looking down!

雞肉鬆脆皮色呈暗紅，
鮮嫩佳餚喜煞兩頑童。

Here Mrs. Bold, her grief still great,
Goes to the cellar with a plate.
She wants a dish of sauerkraut,
And never had she any doubt,
That when she heated up that dish,
It always met her special wish.
But in the meantime, quite aloof,
The boys are busy on the roof.
And Max was clever, for he took
Up to the roof a fishing-hook.

波爾太太悲未消，
手持餐盤下地窖。
要吃一道醃泡菜，
酸辣味濃她最愛。
尤嗜泡菜加熱一招鮮，
入味樂胃從不厭。
頑童小賊屋頂奔忙，
覷覦美食喪心病狂。
麥克斯出歪點子，
拖上釣鉤作工具使。

19 ❧❧

Whoops! - Look here, without hub-bub
A chicken comes already up.
To heave the second was soon done,
To get the third was simply fun.
The fourth gives no more trouble either,
And was no longer left to fry there.

喔唷唷，瞧啊瞧，
悄莫聲兒，一隻烤雞已被釣。
偷取第二隻更容易，
二不過三如兒戲。
第四隻一樣不費事，
一古腦兒偷去吃。

It's true, the little dog did yelp,
He saw it, but he could not help.

小狗見有賊偷雞，
唯有狺狺泄怒氣。

Down the roof they climbed with pleasure,
Mischievous beyond all measure.
This will be a pretty row,
Mrs. Bold is coming now!

頑童喜孜孜溜下屋頂，
真是無與倫比賊精靈。
若被波德太太來追找，
定會大吵又大鬧！

Struck with terror she stops short.
Chickens gone! Oh great good Lord!

波德太太目瞪口呆急止步，
烤雞不翼而飛她暗叫苦。

Unable first a word to utter,
"Pom"! - was all that she could mutter.
"Pom, you beast, what have you done!!
Wait a minute! I'll come!!"

無言之後似恍悟，
只能罵狗拆爛污。

「狗崽子，小畜生，
做的好事，看我怎麼把你整！」

With a ladle him to flog,
She comes down on that poor dog.
He yells loudly, as he knows,
How little he deserves the blows.

操起勺勺使勁打，
她跟小狗要算帳。
汪汪哀號狗叫屈，
錯罰忠良直彎曲。

Snoring in their hiding place
They lie there with upturned face,
And of all the feasting bout
One last bone is peeping out.
This was now the second trick,
And the third will follow quick.

小賊這會兒可愜意，
仰臥打鼾藏身地。
飽餐一頓成隆腹，
嘴裡猶啣一雞骨。
二次惡作劇說到此，
旋即又有第三次。

Third Trick

There was a man whose name was Bray,
He was well known, as I can say.
Workday coats of any sort,
Sunday jackets long and short,
Coats with pockets well designed,
Gaiters, cloaks, skilfully lined,
All these things for people's sake
Mr. Bray knew how to make.
For cutting gowns he had no match,
Or sewing on some hole a patch,
A button lost or loose somewhere
Was quickly fixed and in repair.
Whatever mending there may be,
In front or back or down the knee,
All this was done by Mr. Bray,
And he was busy every day.
As tailoring was his life's end,
So everybody was his friend.
But Max and Maurice were not sick
Of playing here another trick.

Before the tailor's house, quite near,
A brook flowed by there fast and clear.

惡作劇之三

有個漢子叫布雷,
遠近聞名人敬佩。
上班常服式樣多,
週日上衣長短更繁瑣。
帶袋時裝新大衣,
更有襪套斗篷縫夾裡。
布雷縫紉衣物最拿手,
贏得顧客稱讚不絕口。
縫製長袍是絕活,
打個補丁他也做。
釘綴鈕扣他手腳快,
小縫小補也不推卸。
破舊部位不計較,
不管是前襟、背部還是膝部布料。
布雷先生事無巨細必親躬,
真是個無日不忙的好縫工。
人生在世為成衣,
顧客個個是知己。
唯有麥克斯和毛里斯,
又來對他把詭計施。
布雷屋旁有小溪,
溪水清澈又湍急。

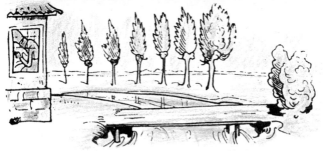

A simple board across the ditch
Was serving as a little bridge.

平平常常小木條，
橫跨溪水當座橋。

Now Max and Maurice had no awe,
They came along there with a saw,
And secretly, this naughty chap
Slit in the bridge a dangerous gap.

無法無天兩頑童，
取來鋸子逞頑凶。
偷偷摸摸興妖風，
橋板鋸出一裂縫。

27 ✧✧✧

When this was done, upon my word,
A sudden shout nearby was heard:
"Tailor, tailor, billygoat,
Hurrah, come out, patch up my coat!"
John Bray could suffer anything,
But when the boys that song did sing,
It always went against the grain,
Which for a tailor is quite plain.

布下陷阱要害人，
近處突然傳響聲：
「裁縫，裁縫，公山羊，
快快出來給大爺補衣裳！」
布雷先生什麼都能忍，
唯有這兒歌最傷人。
裁縫對此最忌諱，
布雷本性不容毀。

Within a minute and not more,
He crossed the threshold of his door
Again he heard that cheeky shout,
That "billygoat" quite near and loud.

裁縫聞聲頓時拂袖起，
一腳跨出門檻尋仇敵。
有人又叫「公山羊」，
聲在近處，真切又響亮。

Plump! On the bridge he jumps and - smash!
It breaks in two with fearful crash.

蹬蹬兩步跳上橋，
咔嚓一聲木板變斷橋。

And what you all along have feared,
The tailor - plop - has disappeared.

讀者諸君必料到，
撲通落水，裁縫把殃遭。

But just as this had happened here
A pair of geese were swimming near.

不遲不早事湊巧，
一對天鵝游弋在近旁。

Bray, scared to death, in his great need,
Gripped now his hands around their feet.
And both the geese tight in his hands,
He flies with them and safely lands.

行將滅頂嚇破膽，
忙把天鵝腳緊攀。
兩鳥拽得布雷騰空起，
飛行半天又穩穩落地。

Of course, he does not feel at ease,
And getting cold, he starts to sneeze.

折騰再三自然不順氣，
中了風寒開始打噴嚏。

By this adventure as was plain,
His stomach also caused him pain.

驚險遭遇遺惡果，
胃痛擾得他好難過。

All praise deserves here Mrs. Bray!
A flat-iron, which she did lay
On his cold belly, safe and sound,
Has brought her poor, sick husband round.

布雷太太真是智多星，
取來平底熨斗專治病。
熨斗移過冷肚皮，
丈夫立時醒轉回過氣。

The news went soon from door to door:
"Good Mr. Bray is well once more."
This was now the third bad trick,
But the fourth will follow quick.

挨家挨戶傳聞揚：

「布雷先生已無恙。」

第三次惡作劇害更重，

叵料劣蹟有四不旋踵。

Fourth Trick

There is a statement and a rule,
Man has to learn some things at school.
Not alone the A-B-C
For knowledge is the only key,
Besides of that is writing, reading
For human mind a useful feeding.
Then you must learn arithmetic,
To it with eagerness should stick,
And likewise you must in full measure
Absorb all wisdom with great pleasure.
To teach all this as an example,
This was the job of teacher Lample.
For Max and Maurice it was sure,
That things of that sort were but poor;
Since boys, who are such naughty creatures,
Will never listen to the teachers.

惡作劇之四

常言道：
求知識在學校。
不但要學字母表，
那是為了求知需鎖鑰；
更要學習寫字和識字，
以為人腦供良智。
算術也是必修課，
堅持不懈學矻矻。
除此之外科目尚多，
好學生當全力以赴。
話說模範教師叫蘭普，
循循善誘不辭辛苦。
兩個頑童是劣等生，
學業從來不認真。
調皮成性愛搗蛋，
不聽師訓無忌憚。

To this brave teacher, every night,
His good old pipe gave much delight.
When all day's drudgery was done,
Tobacco smoking was his fun.
And readily we grant him this,
It was, no doubt, a modest bliss.
But Max and Maurice, never sick,
Were thinking of another trick.
And in their minds the plan was ripe,
To cause him trouble through his pipe.

老師夜夜抽煙斗，
吞雲吐霧逍遙遊。
一日教務夠辛勞，
鬆懈身心靠煙草。
鑒於教師事繁瑣，
這點嗜好不為過。
唯有麥克斯和毛里斯，
永不疲倦動壞心思。
胸有成竹擬計謀，
施行詭計靠煙斗。

When Sunday now came round again,
And Lample at his organ then,
Was sitting there absorbed in playing,
To his communion's pious praying,

此日又逢星期天，
聖餐祈禱最普遍。
蘭普潛心又虔誠，
聖樂伴奏彈風琴。

The naughty boys, without much shame,
Hush-hush into his room then came.
When Max saw here the clay pipe stand
He took it quickly in his hand;

頑童再不存良知，
偷入房間戲教師。
麥克斯見了陶土煙斗，
一把抓來握在手。

But Maurice had another task,
Gunpowder had he in his flask.
He filled the bowl up to the brink,
Of mortal risk he did not think. -
The service being over now,
They hurried home to make no row.

毛里斯另外有分工，
攜來獵人火藥筒，
粒狀火藥塞煙斗，
生死後果不思謀。
禮拜做完教眾散，
頑童悄悄把家還。

And Lample then, his duty done,
Has locked the church, and has begun

To saunter home with music books,
With innocent and peaceful looks.
Anticipating calm and rest
Which he at home found always best.

蘭普盡責行禮畢，
鎖上教堂回家去休息。

挾著樂譜信步走，
臉色安詳又無愁。
家中氣氛最寧靜，
好好休息蓄銳養精。

Well-balanced as it was his type,
He lighted now his good old pipe.

生活作息有規矩，
點燃煙斗享雅趣。

"It's true", he said, "there is no action
That could compare to satisfaction."

「真不假，」蘭普說，
「知足常樂最瀟脫。」

Bang!! - The teacher's pipe is rent,
And with it the room is sent
In a furnace of explosion
And destruction beyond all notion.
Armchair, inkstand, glass, and cup,
All these things go flying up.

轟的一聲如放砲，
煙斗炸裂房屋搖。
爆炸破壞大無比，
桌椅杯瓶全飛起，

When at last the reek was lifting,
And the smoke away was drifting,
Lample was seen lying there,
Alive! - but he had got his share.

待到硫磺臭味散，
房內濃煙不再瀰漫，
只見蘭普地上躺，
大難不死卻受了傷。

Nose, and hands, and ears, and face
Black as niggers by this blaze,
And the last tuft of his hair
Is burnt down and left him bare.

鼻子耳朵和手臉，
燻得猶如黑墨塗個遍。
最後一綹髮，
燒得精光無可拔。

Who shall sit at Lample's stool,
Teach the children now at school?
Who should do for Mr. Lample
Other duties for example?
Out of what could he now smoke,
When the pipe was gone and broke?

誰來接替蘭普職，
教誨學童學知識？
別的工作也不少，
更有誰人可代勞？
陶土煙斗已粉碎，
再無煙具供他求陶醉。

Time heals wounds of any sort,
Save the pipe was not restored.
This was now the fourth bad trick,
But the fifth will follow quick.

時間可治各創傷，
唯有煙斗不能成原狀。
惡作劇之四敘到此，
尚有第五椿接踵至。

Fifth Trick

Who, in village or in town,
Has an uncle settled down,
Polite and modest he should be,
For this the uncle likes to see.
"Good morning", say, "how do you do,
Today what can I do for you?"
Bring him the paper, pipe, and spill,
And be obedient to his will.
If something pinches, bites or nips,
In back or in between the ribs,
Then be obliging any day,
And help him then without delay.
Or if the uncle's taking snuff,
And sneezes loud, caused by this stuff,
Then say - "Bless you", as people do,
"Thanks very much." - "Good luck to you!"
Or he comes home, and it is late,
To pull his boots off do not wait,
Fetch him the slippers, robe, and cap,
Before he takes a little nap.
In short take always utmost care
And be of jobs like these aware.

But Max and Maurice, they indeed,
On such jobs never were agreed,
And only think what fearful dread
They once had caused to uncle Fred.

惡作劇之五

不論鄉俗或城規，
叔伯舅舅是長輩。
侄甥侍奉應周到，
討得長者喜眉梢。
譬如早晨見了要請安，
殷勤動問可有事代辦。
報紙、煙斗和紙捻子，
恭順奉上勿滯遲。
長輩身上痛或癢，
不管哪個部位生微恙，
務必即刻盡孝不得誤，
使他舒心不再痛苦。
要是叔伯用鼻煙，
抽搐鼻子噴嚏連連，
聞聲應按習俗求吉利，
說聲「長命百歲」「保佑你！」
有時叔伯回家遲，
趕快上前幫他脫靴子，
再去拿來拖鞋、睡袍和睡帽，
讓他可以睡一覺。
總而言之小輩時刻要費心，
無微不至盡孝心。

話說麥克斯和毛里斯，
從不侍奉長者的壞小子。
這兒只說一件事，
弗雷特叔叔曾被氣得半死。

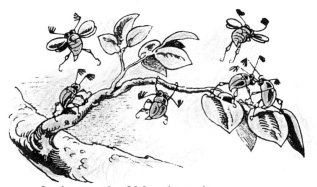

In the month of May the cock-
Chafers often come in flock.
In the trees, and shrubs, and all
They would fly then, creep and crawl.

那是一個五月天，
金龜子群集成一片。
上樹入叢到處是，
鑽啊爬啊還鼓翅。

Max and Maurice, as you see,
Shake them merrily from the tree.
And they put them, crickety-cracks,
In two empty paper-bags.

麥克斯與毛里斯，
樹上搖落金龜子。
一隻一隻捉出來，
塞進兩個空紙袋。

Now they hide the beetles brown
Under uncle's eiderdown.

兩人來到叔叔的鴨絨床，
掀起墊子把甲蟲藏。

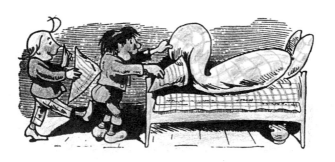

Here you see good uncle Fred
Yawning, - going to his bed.

弗雷特叔叔打哈欠，
上床準備去睡眠。

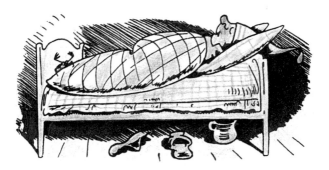

He shuts his eyes and falls asleep,
And soon his rest is good and deep.

閉上雙眼入夢鄉，
睡得深沈又酣暢。

But the beetles, one, two, three,
Are crawling from the mattress free.

一隻一隻甲殼蟲，
紛紛爬出床墊來逞凶。

And the first, which is quite close,
Now takes hold of uncle's nose.

第一隻帶頭爬上前，
咬住老叔鼻子驚好眠。

"Ugh!" - cries he - "What's on my nose?"
And starts up from deep repose.

「喔唷唷！」睡中驚醒他大叫，
「什麼東西把我鼻子咬？」

Horrorstricken, he now fled
In a trice out of his bed.

一看滿床蟲子魂不附體，

一骨碌便從床上跳起。

"Pooh!" - a beast is on his neck
And another on his leg.

「呸！」原來有一蟲附頸項，

另有一隻爬腿上。

All the beetles humming, flying,
Round about, it was most trying.

蟲子嗡嗡繞他飛，

心煩意亂不成寐。

Uncle Fred, quite out of breath,
Tramples all of them to death.

踏死甲蟲在床前，
弗雷特叔叔氣喘連連。

When the beetles were all routed,
Uncle Fred was glad about it.

討厭的蟲子遭全殲，
弗雷特叔叔始釋然。

All the beasts now being slain,
He could sleep and rest again.
This was now the fifth bad trick,
And the sixth will follow quick.

再無蟲子煩擾他，
總算得以歸臥榻。
此乃壞事第五椿，
復有惡行連接上。

Sixth Trick

惡作劇之六

When Eastertime comes round again
The bakers all are busy then.
Of making tarts they never tire,
For everybody's heart's desire.
Max and Maurice liked such sweets,
And were thinking of new deeds.

又是復活節來臨，
糕餅師傅最辛勤。
過節人人喜佳品，
師傅不倦烤餡餅。
兩個頑童嗜甜食，
靈機一動把計使。

But the baker, with great care,
Locked his shop, as you see there.

糕餅師傅細心人，
進出餅屋必鎖門。

So if you want to steal today,
The chimney is the only way.

頑童若要行偷盜。
唯有煙囪作通道。

Black and covered all with soot
They are now from head to foot.

從頭到腳蒙煤灰，
頑童頓成小黑鬼。

Puff! They fall now quite abreast
In a full-filled flour chest.

噗的一聲，兩人並排往下摔，
一頭栽進麵粉櫃。

Through the baker's room they walk,
Round about as white as chalk.

黑鬼頃刻變成白粉人，
尋找糕餅吃現成。

Suddenly, to their delight,
Of bretzels on a shelf get sight.

賊眼溜溜四處轉，
喜見架上有煎餅捲。

The chair gives way, they tumble off,

椅子坍塌人跌跤，

And they are lying in the trough.

不偏不倚摔進揉麵槽。

Wrapped in dough quite snug and tight,
They present a pitious sight.

沾黏生麵團，活像套上緊身衣，
兩人模樣真滑稽。

69

And what everybody fears,
Master baker now appears.

合該這天要出事，
那廂走來糕餅師。

Before a further word was said,
He rolls them into loaves of bread.

不由分說用力揉，
生坯兩圍出巧手。

The baker's oven still a-glow,
He shoves them in as loaves of dough.

烤爐膛裡火熊熊，
推進活人當麵包烘。

Here from the oven crisp and brown,
They are now taken and set down.

烤得鬆脆又焦黃，
新鮮麵包出爐膛。

While everybody thinks them dead,
They are not really done for yet.

都以為此番劫數難逃，
誰知頑童命大出意料。

And nibbling just like little mice
They find the pastry good and nice.

活像兩隻小耗子，
嘔吧嘔吧把噴香的麵包吃。

The bakerman can only shout -
"Good gracious! They are running out!"
This was now their sixth bad trick,
But the last will follow quick.

糕餅師傅只會大聲叫：
「老天！兩個麵人脫了殼跑掉！」
惡作劇之六到此了結，
且聽下回再分解。

Last Trick

最後一次惡作劇

Max and Maurice, just you wait,
This trick is to be your fate!

麥克斯和毛里斯等著瞧,
這回惡貫滿盈再難逃!

Those two rogues could not abstain
From cutting slits in sacks of grain.

兩個壞蛋手癢癢,
劃破麻袋去偷糧。

Here you see the farmer Jack
Carrying a heavy malting sack.

農夫傑克弓著腰，
扛袋去把麥芽泡。

But no sooner does he go,
Than the corn begins to flow.

不曾走出兩三步，
麥粒漏出地下鋪。

His surprise is very great:
"Damn, that thing is loosing weight!"

莫明所以他驚叫：
「見鬼，這袋子怎得輕飄飄！」

Turning presently his face,
He spots them in their hiding place,

轉過臉來看究竟，

看見頑童匿身形。

And shovels instantly the pair
In his sack with gleeful care.

甕中捉鱉逮流氓，

Being taken to the mill,
Max and Maurice, both feel ill.

捆賊裝袋奔磨坊，
一對頑童暗神傷。

"Good morning, miller, how d'you do?
I have some business here for you!"

「早安，我的磨坊主，
有點東西請你磨一磨！」

Out with them, to pay their bill,
The rogues are poured into the mill.

欠債筆筆心頭記，
一對惡棍被倒進碾磨機。

Turning now with creaks and groans
Grind the miller's two big stones.

嘰哩嘎啦大石磨，
開動起來碾出粉末多。

Ground to pieces here you might
Get of them a last sad sight.

最後見到的小頑童，
便是這樣的兩攤骨屑和肉鬆。

And the miller's ducks enjoy,
What is left of either boy.

磨坊主的鴨子走來，
美美享受兩殘骸。

End

When the news now spread abroad,
Of mourning no one really thought.
Said Mrs. Bold, she was not wrong,
"Haven't I known it all along?"
"There you are!" said Mr. Bray
"Wickedness ends in decay!"
"Well", declared the teacher Lample,
"This again is an example!"
"A sweet-tooth, well, has many a man!"
Asserted our bakerman.
And even our uncle Fred
Had hardly any tears to shed.
The farmer also took that line:
"Why, it's no business of mine!"
In the whole place round about
People now were glad to shout:
"Thank God, the village is now cured
Of evils we have long endured!!"

尾聲

消息一經傳播開，
無人願為頑童致哀。
波爾太太自稱早知曉：
「這樣的結局早意料！」
「你們瞧！」布雷先生開了腔，
「作惡多端終無好下場！」
蘭普老師愛宣講：
「以儆效尤的壞榜樣！」
糕餅師傅講實際：
「愛吃甜食的人該把教訓記！」
還有老叔弗雷特，
不揮一淚心安又理得。
農夫的態度肖大家，
連稱此事與己無涉不怪他。
左鄰右舍眾鄉親，
聞訊無不額手稱慶：
「感謝仁慈的上帝，
除去長期為害的惡少福鄉里！」

The Fly
蒼蠅

The good inspector thinks it's best
To have at noon a little rest.

警長大人好福氣，
日日午睡養身體。

A fly is coming now quite near
And buzzes loudly round his ear.

嗡嗡飛來一蒼蠅，
圍著耳朵轉悠近。

And being roused from gentle slumbing,
He looks morosely at that humming.

淺淺小盹被擾亂，
睡眼惺忪鬱不歡。

The nasty fly, to find a bed,
Exactly perched on his bald head.

可惡的蒼蠅要棲停，
瞄準禿頂落下叮。

"Now wait a minute, cheeky beast,
I'll no longer being teased."

「好個蒼蠅逞猖狂，
等我給你一巴掌。」

He sneaks now gently to the cup,
To catch it there without hubbub.

看見杯口蒼蠅趴，
不聲不響上前要把害蟲抓。

Sport as he was, he knew to land,
He has it really in his hand.

雖然笨拙常被人笑，
一把抓住蒼蠅捏得牢。

And now he looks with cunning eye,
Where it may hide, the nasty fly.

眯縫眼睛看究竟，
掌中何處藏蒼蠅。

Hurray! It's free among the clatter,
One leg, that is of little matter.

忙亂之中蒼蠅逃，
手中只留細腿一條。

He was now trying with a flap,
If he could kill it with one clap,

再用蠅拍試揮掃，
一擊成功是絕招。

And to be sure now, in his flare.
Was climbing on the easy-chair.

這回不能再失手，
爬上椅子怒在心頭。

The chair gives way and there they lie,
While happily escapes the fly.

不料椅子一打滑，
人仰馬翻抓個瞎。

But now he swings his arm with strength,
The fly is put to death at length.

再次掄臂打個正著，
蒼蠅終於一命嗚呼歸陰曹。

How glad he was of this effect,
To be released of that insect.

慶幸自己功已成，
蒼蠅不能再擾人。

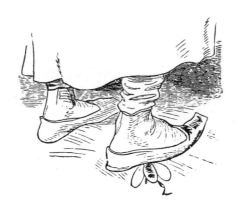

Refreshing is a nap at noon,
But often you are grudged this boon.

午睡縱然養精神，
卻也並非日日保安寧。

The Raven's Nest

鴉巢

Two boys, quite young and in high glee,
Come with a ladder, as you see.

兩個男孩年紀小，
頑皮搬來梯一條。

"To catch young ravens is great fun",
Says one of them, "it's easily done."

「摸巢捉鳥最好玩，」
一個男童說，「這事一點也不難。」

The ladder falls, and so each boy,
The ravens watch it with great joy.

梯子一歪男童往下摔，
巢中烏鴉見了喜開懷。

They topple over from the tree,
Their legs are all that you can see.

頭朝下雙雙跌進臭水塘，
唯有腿腳露面上。

A huntsman comes now to this bog,
"Go on and fetch", cries to his dog.

獵人走到水塘邊，
驅狗下水把人唧。

One boy is carried like a snipe,
Whereas the hunter smokes his pipe.

獵狗唧起一個似叼鳥，
獵人點上煙斗看熱鬧。

"Now fetch the other from the bog!"
But he sneaks off, the cunning dog.

「再去水塘把另個救！」
獵狗狡懶偷偷溜。

The hunter takes himself the trouble
To drag the boy from mud and bubble.

獵人無奈自己動手，
拖著男孩出了泥水和污垢。

The half of them completely black,
Like ravens the two rogues come back.

半身墨黑似烏鴉，
兩童扛梯再來把樹爬。

Black are the hunter's boots you see,
So are the dog's up to his knee.

獵人雙靴沾滿泥，
小狗膝蓋以下皆黑皮。

The ravens in their nest, however,
They danced with joy, and cried: "I never!"

巢中烏鴉齊嘿嘿，
跳舞嗤笑別人黑。

Diogenes And The Boys Of Corinth

狄俄涅斯和科林斯的男孩

Meditating in his tun,
Diogenes lies in the sun.

身藏酒桶作冥想，
狄俄涅斯曬太陽。

A boy who saw him lying here
Waves to his friend, who is quite near.

男孩見到酒桶裡面躺個人，
招手喚來朋友鬧一陣。

The rascals now begin a tapping,
And on the tun a constant rapping.

手指篤篤敲酒桶，
扣擊聲聲入耳窿。

Diogenes looks out of door,
And be disturbed, says: "What's that for?"

狄俄涅斯探出頭，
驚擾休息問緣由。

Malicious is the one and pert,
Goes where he finds a water squirt.

一個童子好捉狹，
水槍射水作戲耍。

He spirts the water through the hole,
Diogenes gets wet, poor soul.

穿口入桶水噴射，
狄俄涅斯頓濕透。

No sooner was he in the tun,
When both boys try another fun.

待到再進酒桶藏，
二孩又來取樂忙。

They roll the tun and give no peace,
"Stop, stop", cries now Diogenes.

兩人推得酒桶滾前進，
只聽狄俄涅斯連叫「停」。

He gets quite giddy in his tun,
Look out! The punishment will come!

滾得頭昏又眼花，
注意！報應從來非空話！

For what at first they never thought,
Their jackets by two nails were caught.

搗蛋鬼們未料到，
衣服竟被釘子鉤牢。

"Help, help!" the frightened boys cry out,
And rolling kick their legs about.

兩個孩子狂呼救命，
酒桶滾滾雙腿亂蹬。

Their weeping, crying was in vain,
What happened to them is now plain.

哭叫再三全無用，
結局已在意料中。

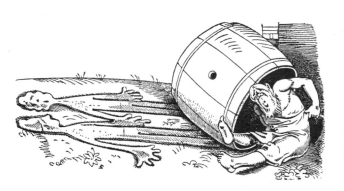

Alas, by that big, weighty vat,
Like strudel-dough, they are rolled flat.

可憐龐然大物壓過身，
活人像個麵團碾扁平。

Diogenes says in his tun,
"Thus always ends excessive fun."

狄俄涅斯鑽回大酒桶：
「樂極生悲無善終。」

The Two Ducks And The Frog

兩隻鴨子和青蛙

It's clear what these two duckies want,
Which slowly waddle to the pond.

兩隻小鴨性頑皮，
搖搖擺擺到水塘去遊戲。

Into the water here with glee
They dive their heads, as you can see.

埋頭入水搖屁股，
清涼舒適隨波浮。

And one had luck, for it has found
A green frog, hidden in the ground.

一鴨忽得好運氣，
找到青蛙擬充飢。

Of course, she thought this frog is mine,
But here she failed in her design.

「青蛙自然應歸我。」
計謀不成急死鴨婆。

The duck, and so her mate the drake,
Extend the frog on either leg.

公鴨要來分食青蛙,
兩鴨各咬一腿亂撕拉。

When crosswise torn he almost faints,
So ghastly did he feel the pains.

蛙身拉作十字形，
幾近昏厥痛難禁。

Now like a man the frog fights well,
If he succeeds, no one can tell.

垂死掙扎蛙躍起，
要跟鴨子鬥高低。

The head is in, the frog is shocked,
The grim duck's throat, however, locked.

公鴨吞進青蛙頭，
不進不出卡喉頭。

And when the two ducks have a fight,
The frog has got an easy flight.

兩鴨爭奪美食急，
青蛙乘機溜之大吉。

At last, they try to recollect,
If in the well could be detect.

醒悟過來奔水井，
且看有否蛙藏身。

When looking through the water pipe,
They head no chance the frog to gripe.

青蛙穿過水管急逃命，
兩鴨在後追趕緊。

The ducks were cackling through the grate,
To catch the frog was now too late.

鴨頭伸出欄柵嘎嘎叫，
眼看青蛙捕不到。

He had escaped, what shall I say,
The ducks, too, wished to fly away.

青蛙劫後得餘生，
輪到鴨子求脫身。

But soon the cook was there, you see,
"Ha-ha", he laughs, "now come with me".

不料走來胖廚師，
喜捉雙鷗去把佳餚治。

Three weeks the frog was laid up then!
Thank heaven, now he smokes again!

青蛙養傷繃帶纏頭，
三星期後又見他抽煙斗！

Eginhard and Emma
艾琴哈和艾瑪

A Carnival Comedy in Pictures
狂歡節的喜劇

Carolus Magnus creeps quite deep,
Into his bed, he wants to sleep.

查理大帝上臥榻，
只求美美睡個暢。

But caused by those wild Saxons' rout,
He is afflicted with a gout.

大帝苦於痛風病，
皆因薩克遜人喜宴飲。

The night is long, much aches his knee,
He practises the A B C

漫漫長夜膝痛苦，
只好坐起練習寫字母。

Another fit like that before!
He flings the slateboard on the floor.

又是一陣大發作，
丟下書寫板苦偈促。

Old Fred appears, called by the bell,
"Give me a rub, that gout's like hell!"

打鈴召來老僕弗雷特：

「給我按摩，不然痛得寡人睡不得！」

And Frederick says: "I thought as much,
The snow outside caused this bad touch."

弗雷特說：「老僕料到陛下苦，
屋外雪大自然使你痛徹骨。」

"What", cries Carolus, "that's a shame",
And kicks his servant almost lame.

「什麼話！」大帝勃發雷霆怒，
一腳踢翻多嘴的老奴。

When going out, Fred's gait was slow,
The king looks out to see the snow.

弗雷特一瘸一拐慢步跨，
大帝探身窗外看雪花。

What did he see, when looking hard?
Young Emma carries Eginhard.

定睛一看發大怒，
只見艾瑪把艾琴哈背上馱。

He calls the guard, "now take good care,
Go out and catch the naughty pair".

他向衛士下命令：

「給我抓住這對賤人。」

And so their flight, soon by the guard,
Was hampered here for Eginhard.

衛士唧命忙橫戟，
艾琴哈逃跑被攔截。

When they were ushered in a line,
The king with dignity gave a sign.

兩人魚貫被押進，

大帝威嚴揮手發號令

Though they kneel down without a sound,
The king refrained from turning round.

青年男女恭順急下跪，
大帝不肯轉身屈尊貴。

But suddenly no more enraged,
In tears he said: "Be now engaged!"

情緒突變大帝忽含淚：
「寡人允你倆配成對！」

All's well that ends well!
諸事終有良局配。

Note: Eginhard or Einhard (770 - 840) was the famous biographer of the life of Charles the Great (742 - 814). Living at the court of the Emperor and being in constant touch with him, he was able to delineate every detail of his sovereign's life in his biography "Vita Caroli Magni". He was married to Emma, the sister of the bishop of Worms; but according to an old story or saga, his wife was the secret daughter of Charles the Great, who really had an offspring of the same name. So as this love affair had to be concealed, it happened that one night, in winter, Emma carried her lover on her back through the snow to prevent Eginhard's footprints from being detected. This narrative is the background of W. Busch's funny cartoons.

注釋：艾琴哈（770—840），亦作艾恩哈，是撰寫查理大帝（742—814）傳記的著名作家。他生活在大帝的宮廷中，並與大帝接觸頻繁，因而得以在傳記作品《查理大帝一生》中，細緻描繪這位君主的生活。他娶渥姆斯主教之妹艾瑪為妻，但根據一則古老的傳說或傳奇，其妻是查理大帝秘而不宣的女兒，而大帝確也有女名叫艾瑪。由於這段姻緣必須保守秘密，據說冬日某夜，艾瑪在雪地上曾背負自己的愛人而行，以免讓人看到艾琴哈的腳印。這段故事為W・勃希的漫畫作品提供了背景依據。

三民 廣解英漢辭典 精裝本／1400元

大專、高中學生及深造者的好搭檔

⊕收錄各種專門術語、時事用語10萬字
⊕收集坊間前所未收的新字，切合需要

三民 新英漢辭典 精裝本／900元

在學及進修者的寶典

⊕翻譯及重點標示簡單明瞭
⊕附錄「英文文法總整理」，查閱方便